DISNEY PRINCESS

5-Minute Princess Stories

DISNEY PRESS

Los Angeles • New York

Contents

Cinderella

The Lost Mice

One clear winter night, the Prince led Cinderella out to the balcony.

"I have a surprise for you," he said, handing her a box.

Inside was a beautiful new coat. "Oh, it's simply lovely!" Cinderella exclaimed. "Thank you!"

It was a pretty and thoughtful gift. The coat would keep her warm during the cold weather.

The next morning, the princess showed her coat to Suzy, one of her mouse friends. "Isn't the Prince thoughtful?" Cinderella remarked.

"Nice-a! Nice-a!" Suzy exclaimed. The coat sleeve felt warm and cozy—especially compared to where the mice lived.

A few minutes later, Jaq and Gus went into Cinderella's room. It had been a chilly night in the attic, and the mice were still shivering.

"Cinderelly! Cinderelly!" Jaq called. He knew that if he told the princess how cold the attic was, she would do something about it. But she was rushing off to get dressed for a tea party, so she didn't hear her friend.

3

Jaq sighed. It was too cold for the mice to stay in the attic much longer. Cinderella had always been very kind to the mice, and Jaq was sure she would want them to be warm.

So he and Gus called the rest of the mice down from the attic. They sat in front of a blazing fire in Cinderella's room. Before long, their cold paws and tails had warmed up, and their teeth stopped chattering. They'd wait there until Cinderella got back.

Soon, the new housekeeper came in to clean the room. When she saw the mice, she shrieked and shooed them away. "Mice don't belong in the castle!" she yelled. "Now get out!"

The housekeeper didn't know that the mice were Cinderella's friends. She chased them with a broom. The frightened mice had no choice but to scramble back up to the cold attic.

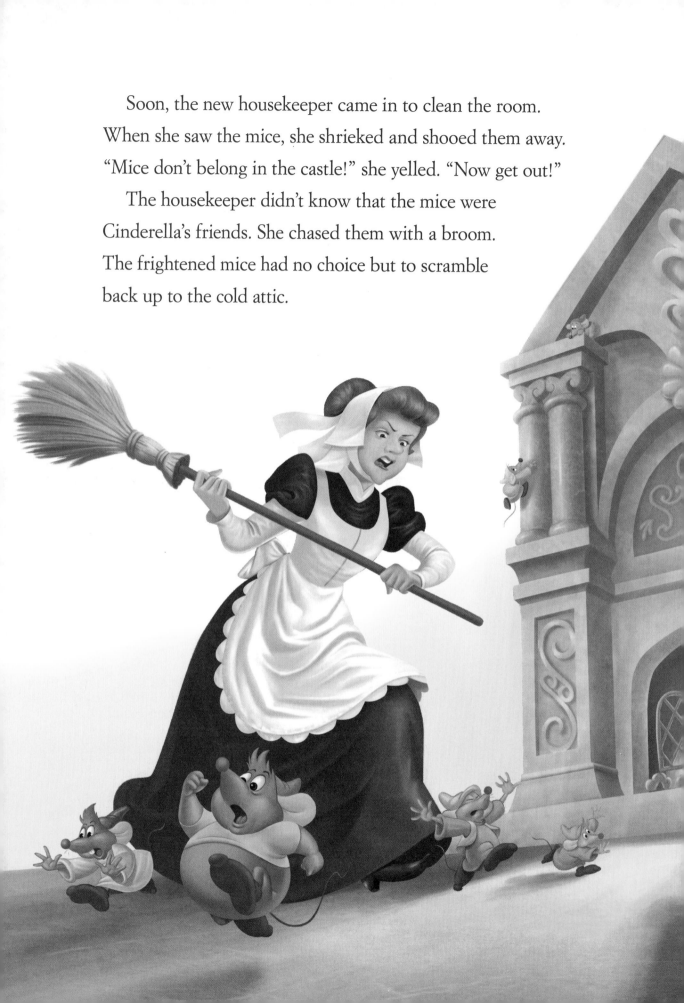

"*Brrrr.*" Gus began to shiver as soon as the mice were safely upstairs.

The mice really needed the princess's help! But how would they be able to speak to Cinderella when they were afraid to set foot downstairs?

WHAM! Suddenly, the castle gardener barged through the attic door. Before the mice knew what was happening, he had trapped them.

"Now take them outside!" they heard the housekeeper say. "Take them far away so they never return!"

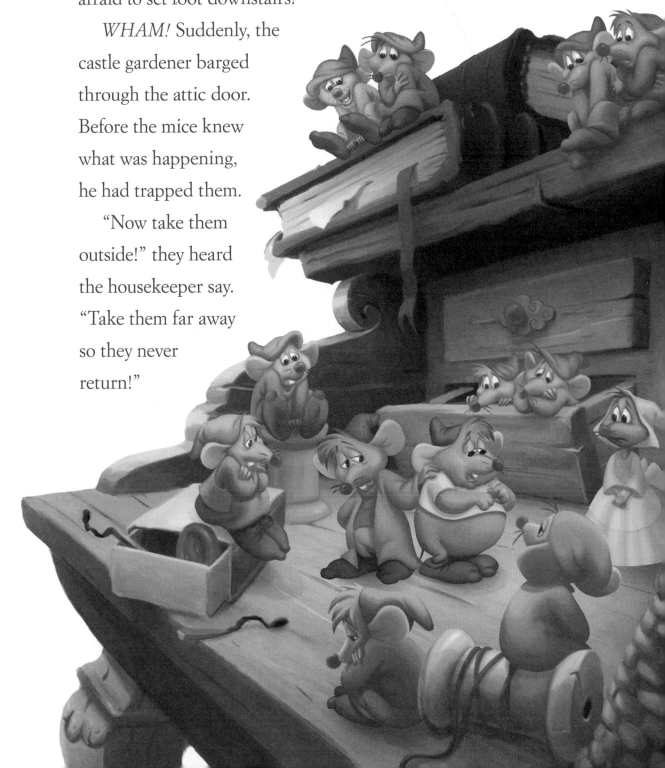

Meanwhile, Cinderella's tea party had ended and she and the Prince were out riding. As their horses trotted through the countryside, they saw the castle gardener tending to something in one of the fields.

"Hello!" the Prince called out. "It's much too cold to be working outside!"

But the gardener did not answer. The Prince called
to him again and still got no reply.

As they rode on, the Prince turned to Cinderella.
"That was odd," he said. "I can't believe he did not hear
me. Why wouldn't he answer?"

"Perhaps he was lost in thought?" Cinderella replied.

Cinderella was right. The gardener had been trying
to make a decision. He was about to let the mice go as the
housekeeper had ordered. But he was worried about them.
He knew it was too cold outside.

Finally, he decided to take the mice to the stables. "Now
don't tell the housekeeper," he told the stable workers. "But
these poor mice need a warm place to stay and a bite to eat."

The mice were very grateful to their new friends.

The mice nestled together in the barn. But as night approached, the stables got colder. Luckily, the horses were very friendly. They told the mice to snuggle in their manes to keep warm.

"Thassa nice-a," said Gus as he drifted off to sleep.

Later that night, back at the castle, Cinderella was starting to worry. She hadn't seen the mice since that morning. Jaq and Gus nearly always came by in the evening.

Cinderella was searching for the mice when she ran into the Prince.

"Why, hello!" the Prince said. "Are you looking for the same person I am?"

"Why, no, I don't think so," Cinderella replied. "I'm looking for the mice!"

"Ah," said the Prince. "Well, I am looking for our new housekeeper. Apparently she threw the mice out of the castle today!"

"Oh, no!" Cinderella cried. "Poor dears. They'll freeze outside!"

"Don't worry," the Prince said. "The mice have found a new friend." He told Cinderella about what the gardener had done.

Together, Cinderella and the Prince went to the
stables. They thanked the gardener and the stable
workers. Then they gently woke the mice.

"Cinderelly! Cinderelly!" the mice shouted happily.

Cinderella was relieved to see her little friends safe
and sound. Though the stables had been nice, the mice
were glad to return to the castle.

From then on, Cinderella made sure the mice
always had a warm place of their own—in one of the
main rooms of the castle.

A few nights later, Cinderella and the Prince threw a
grand ball. The gardener was the guest of honor. By then, the
housekeeper had been properly introduced to the mice, and all
was well.

As the guests twirled around the dance floor, the mice
celebrated with a banquet of their own, warm and cozy at last.

THE LITTLE MERMAID
A Special Song

"May I have your attention, please?" Sebastian called. The crab tapped his baton on a podium. King Triton's birthday was in a couple of days, and the court musicians were planning a special performance. Triton's daughter, Ariel, would sing while the orchestra played a brand-new tune. Sebastian wanted the concert to be spectacular, but they still had a lot of work to do.

The crab raised his baton, and the musicians began to play. Beautiful music filled the sea, until—*clang!*

"Who did that?" Sebastian demanded.

"Um . . . I did," a young mermaid named Coral replied quietly.

"The best way to play the cymbals is to hold on to them! Now, if there are no more interruptions," Sebastian said grumpily, "let's continue."

The rehearsal went from bad to worse. Coral dropped her cymbal a second time. *Clang!* Then she tripped and landed on top of a kettledrum.

As Ariel watched, Sebastian threw down his baton. "Rehearsal is over!" the crab yelled and stormed off.

Ariel helped Coral up. "Don't mind Sebastian,"

"I'll never be able to get this song right—let alone perfect!"
Coral said sadly.

"Don't worry about it," Ariel said. "The only thing *I'm*
perfect at is making Sebastian mad. You should have seen his
face the last time I went to the surface."

"You've been to the surface?" Coral asked, amazed. "You
must be the bravest mermaid ever!"

"It's just something I like to do," Ariel said. "I'm always
gathering treasures. Would you like to see my collection?"

"I'd love to!" Coral exclaimed.

The two mermaids swam to Ariel's grotto.

"Make yourself at home," Ariel told Coral when they arrived. Flounder the fish was there. He waved a fin at them.

The young mermaid swam around, examining jewelry and shiny trinkets. "Where did you find all of this?" Coral asked as she put on a strand of pearls.

"I found some of it in sunken ships," replied Ariel.

"You've been inside a sunken ship?" Coral said with a gasp. "Weren't you scared?"

"Of course not. Were you, Flounder?" Ariel teased.

"Nothing to it!" the fish fibbed.

"So what are we waiting for?" Ariel asked. "Let's go!"

Coral and Flounder trailed behind Ariel. Soon they arrived at a ship that had sunk to the ocean floor.

"Let's see what's in there!" Ariel urged.

Her friends followed her through a large porthole.

Inside the ship, Ariel found an old steamer trunk. "Look at this!" she cried, holding up a purple parasol.

"And this!" Coral exclaimed, picking up a fancy lamp shade. "I wonder what it's for?"

"My friend Scuttle can tell us," Ariel said. "Follow me!"

"Where are we going?" Coral asked Flounder.

"To the surface," he replied matter-of-factly.

Soon the friends arrived at the surface. Scuttle the seagull examined their treasures. "That is a *twirleriffer*!" he said, looking at Coral's lamp shade. "It's what human ladies wear when they're going somewhere important."

Before long, the friends had to leave.

As they headed home, Coral asked Ariel if she could keep the *twirleriffer* at the grotto. "It might get broken at home," she explained.

"Of course," Ariel agreed. "The grotto is my secret place, and it can be yours, too."

A few days later, as Ariel swam toward the grotto, she heard someone singing. The voice was strong and clear—but sweet, too.

When Ariel arrived, she saw her new friend.

"Coral! I didn't know you had such a lovely voice! You should be singing in the concert, not playing the cymbals."

The little blond mermaid shrugged. "I just like singing to myself," she explained. "I've never actually performed."

The next day at rehearsal, Sebastian made Ariel and
the orchestra practice over and over, but something always
seemed to go wrong.

"The big day is tomorrow!" the crab said, fretting. "This
concert needs to be fit for a king—King Triton, to be exact!
Let's try it again." So they did. The rehearsal went on and on.

By the end of the afternoon, everyone was tired. "See
you tomorrow," Ariel said. Her voice was raspy.

On the day of the concert, Ariel could only whisper. She had lost her voice! Luckily, she knew who could take her place.

"Me?" Coral said when the princess asked her. "But I can't!"

"You must!" Sebastian insisted. "Otherwise King Triton's birthday celebration will be ruined!"

"I can't sing in front of a crowd of merpeople," Coral said, pleading.

"Sure you can," Flounder said.

Coral thought about how she had visited a sunken ship and gone to the surface, things she had never thought she could do—all because of Ariel. Now her new friend was counting on her.

"All right," Coral said slowly. "I'll do it."

That night, when Coral peeked out from backstage, she nearly fainted. The entire kingdom was there—including her parents and her brothers and sisters! King Triton and Ariel sat in the royal box.

When it was time, Coral took a deep breath and swam onstage. As the orchestra started playing, she sang softly. But as she went on, Coral's voice got louder. Before she knew it, the concert was over, and the audience began to clap and cheer.

"Coral," said Sebastian, smiling, "you can give away your cymbals. From now on, you're going to be a court singer!"

After the show, Ariel went to congratulate her friend.
She found Coral with her family.

"I didn't know you could sing like that!" one of Coral's
sisters exclaimed.

"No one ever would have known if it wasn't for Ariel,"
replied Coral. "She believed in me."

Ariel still couldn't speak, but she gave Coral a big hug.
It had been a wonderful evening.

Beauty and the Beast
Belle and the Castle Puppy

Belle was strolling through the castle garden one chilly spring day when she heard a whimpering sound. A puppy was huddled outside the castle gates. He looked cold and dirty.

"Oh, you poor thing!" Belle cried. "Let's get you warmed up and fed!"

She wrapped the puppy in her red cloak and hurried to the castle.

Belle and the enchanted objects gave the puppy a bath.
The coatrack brought a towel.

When he was clean and dry, the puppy ate a bowl of
warm stew.

"He's so cute! I hope we can keep him!" Chip the teacup
exclaimed.

All the enchanted objects were happy to have a guest. But
the ottoman remembered when he had been a real dog, just like
the puppy. What if Belle and the Beast liked this dog better? The
ottoman tried to get the princess's attention. With a funny little
grrr, he raced around the kitchen. But no one noticed.

A moment later, the puppy barked at the door.

"Do you want to go out to play?" Belle asked.

As Belle and the others followed the puppy outside, they
didn't see the ottoman slink out behind them and walk in a
different direction. They laughed as Belle threw sticks for the
puppy to fetch.

The Beast walked up to Belle a while later.

"Someone has dug up my roses!" he exclaimed.

Then the Beast saw the puppy. "Did that dog ruin my garden? Get rid of him—NOW!" the Beast roared as he stomped away.

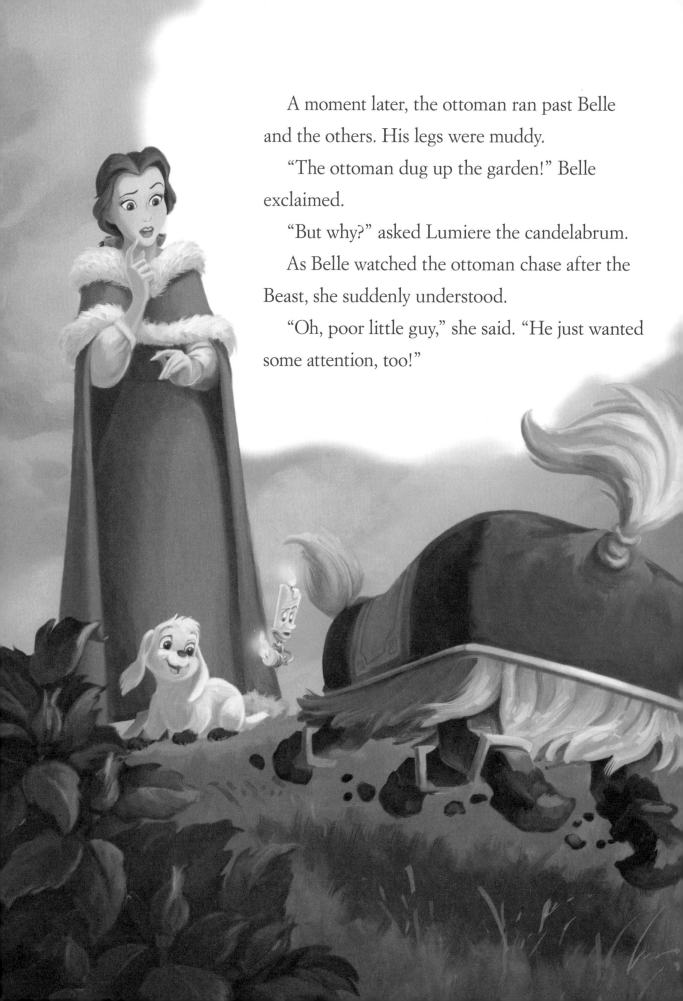

A moment later, the ottoman ran past Belle and the others. His legs were muddy.

"The ottoman dug up the garden!" Belle exclaimed.

"But why?" asked Lumiere the candelabrum.

As Belle watched the ottoman chase after the Beast, she suddenly understood.

"Oh, poor little guy," she said. "He just wanted some attention, too!"

Suddenly, the puppy raced after the ottoman, barking playfully. They both disappeared among the trees.

"What if they don't catch up to the Beast? They'll get lost!" Belle exclaimed. "I have to bring them back safely."

"But it's getting dark," Mrs. Potts protested.

Belle looked at the long shadows creeping through the forest. Clutching her cloak tightly, she took a deep breath and started toward the trees.

"Wait!" Lumiere called to Belle. "I'll come and light your way."

"Thank you," Belle said as she picked up the candelabrum. "I'm glad you're coming."

"Me, too. I think," Lumiere replied. But his flames flickered nervously.

Belle walked along a path. She had come this way before.

"Puppy! Ottoman!" she called.

She hoped that they had met up with the Beast. She was looking forward to returning to the castle.

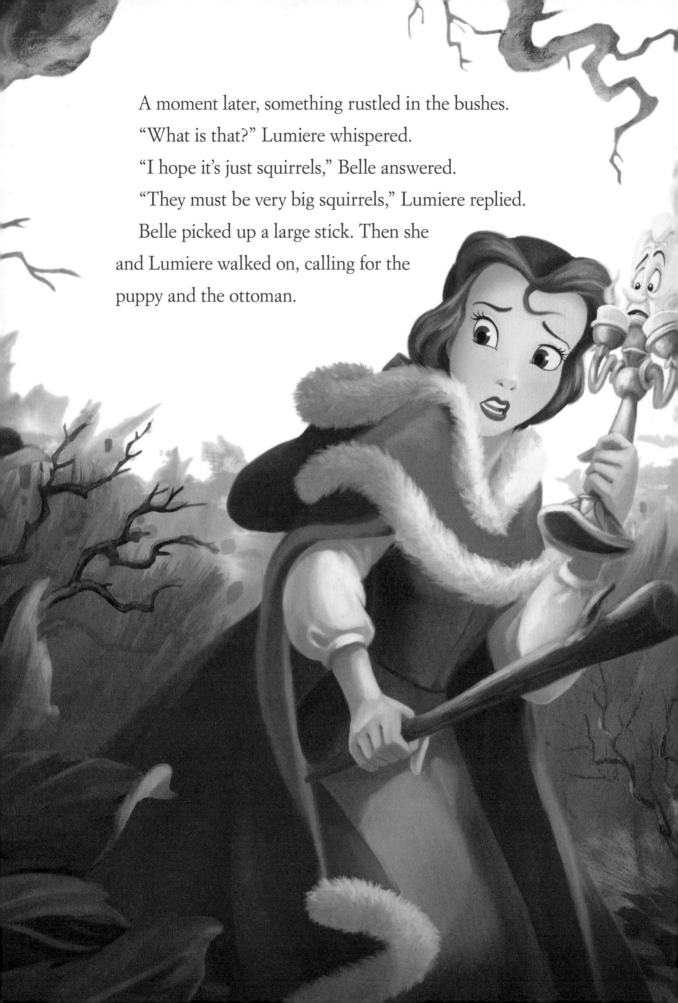

A moment later, something rustled in the bushes.

"What is that?" Lumiere whispered.

"I hope it's just squirrels," Belle answered.

"They must be very big squirrels," Lumiere replied.

Belle picked up a large stick. Then she and Lumiere walked on, calling for the puppy and the ottoman.

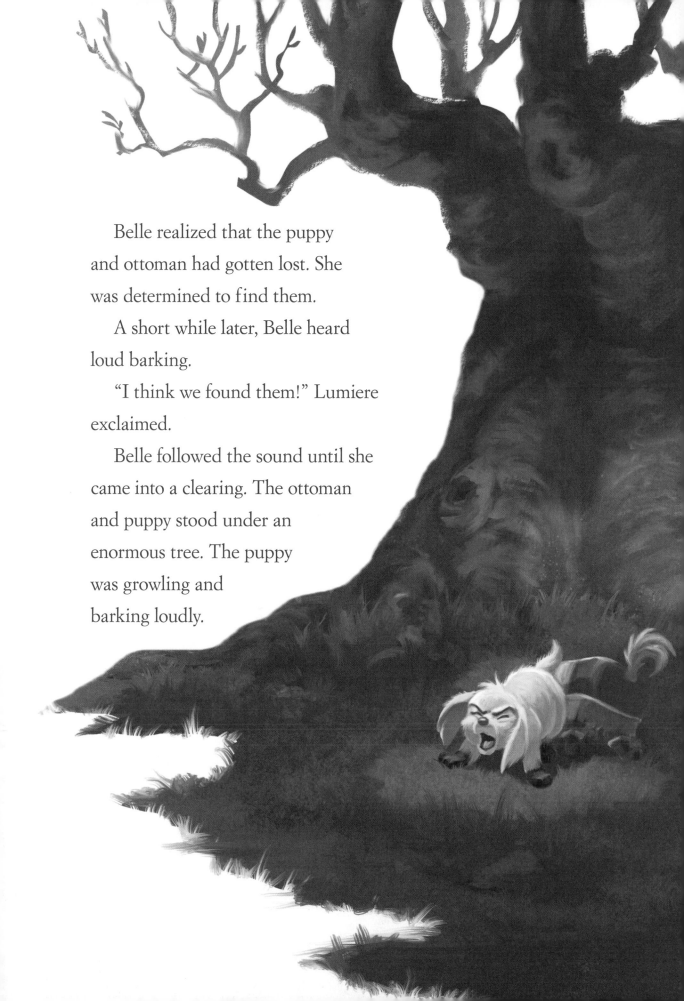

Belle realized that the puppy
and ottoman had gotten lost. She
was determined to find them.

A short while later, Belle heard
loud barking.

"I think we found them!" Lumiere
exclaimed.

Belle followed the sound until she
came into a clearing. The ottoman
and puppy stood under an
enormous tree. The puppy
was growling and
barking loudly.

"What's wrong?" Belle wondered aloud. Then she looked around and gasped. A large wolf was sitting nearby.

"The puppy is protecting the ottoman!" Lumiere exclaimed.

"He's too small to stop that wolf for long," Belle said. "He needs help!"

Quickly, Belle put Lumiere on the ground and lit the stick she had been carrying. She ran toward the wolf, swinging it.

"Get away! Get away!" she shouted.

But the wolf didn't move.

Just then, the Beast showed up. The wolf ran away, yelping with fear.

"The puppy tried to save the ottoman!" Belle told the Beast.

"They are brave little fellows," the Beast answered.

Cradling the puppy in one arm and the ottoman in the other, he led Belle to the castle.

Later that night, everyone settled by the fireplace. Belle watched the Beast stroke the ottoman and feed biscuits to the puppy.

"May the puppy stay until I can find him a home?" she asked.

The Beast cleared his throat. "His home is here—with us," he answered gruffly.

Belle smiled. She was glad that the Beast had come around.

The very next day, the Beast presented the puppy and the ottoman with shiny badges. From now on, they would be the official protectors of the house.

Yip! Yip! Woof! Woof! They couldn't have been more excited.

A Surprise Guest

*I*t was a balmy afternoon in New Orleans—perfect for a night with friends.

"Charlotte, honey!" Big Daddy LaBouff called to his daughter. "How about going to Tiana's Palace for supper tonight?"

"Oh, Daddy, that would be wonderful! Just give me a minute to change."

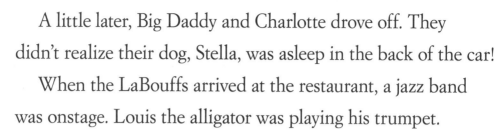

A little later, Big Daddy and Charlotte drove off. They didn't realize their dog, Stella, was asleep in the back of the car!

When the LaBouffs arrived at the restaurant, a jazz band was onstage. Louis the alligator was playing his trumpet.

"Charlotte! How are you?" Princess Tiana exclaimed. She was happy to see her best friend. "Big Daddy, would you like to sit with my mama and Naveen's parents?"

"Why, I can't think of anyone better to share my supper with than Eudora and your in-laws," he replied. Soon Tiana's family and friends were settled at a big table. The princess walked around the dining room to make sure her other guests were happy, too.

Meanwhile, Stella had woken up. The dog climbed out of the LaBouffs' car and looked around. Immediately, she caught the mouthwatering scent of Tiana's beignets. Stella followed her nose right into the restaurant kitchen.

"*Lookee* here!" shouted one of the cooks. "We have a visitor! Here you go, puppy—have some of this gumbo. It's a new recipe."

Stella eagerly tasted the dish. It was delicious! A moment later, a waiter threw her a large bone. The dog couldn't believe her good luck.

Stella spent the whole evening in the kitchen. While Charlotte and Big Daddy dined to Louis's jazz music and talked with their friends, Stella was getting all kinds of treats.

Late that night, after the last jazz number had been played, all of the guests went home. Charlotte and Big Daddy never realized that Stella was also at the restaurant! "Ta-ta!" Charlotte called as they left.

Eudora left with Naveen's parents. Turning to her daughter, she said, "I have never heard the band play quite that well. And that new gumbo—absolutely delicious. I'll see you tomorrow, sweetheart."

After Princess Tiana walked her family to the door, she went back to the dining room to finish cleaning up.

A few minutes later, Louis and the band went to the
kitchen for their evening meal.

As they walked in, Stella began to bark. *Grrr! Woof!*
She was terrified of the giant alligator.

"Oh, now hold on, little dog!" Louis spoke to Stella.
"I'm not here to eat you. I just wanted a taste of the chef's
new gumbo!"

But Stella was frightened. She kept barking.
The kitchen staff and the band members
looked at each other. They weren't sure what to do.

In the dining room, Tiana and Naveen heard the barking. They rushed to see what was causing the commotion.

Tiana recognized the LaBouffs' pet at once. "Stella? What are you doing here?" she asked. "Don't worry. Louis is our friend. He wouldn't hurt anybody."

"That's true!" Naveen cried, putting his arm around Louis. "He is nothing but a big guy with an even bigger heart."

The alligator peeked out from behind his tail. He didn't understand why the dog was so upset.

Stella looked at him suspiciously.

"Go ahead," Princess Tiana encouraged the dog. "Just go over and make friends."

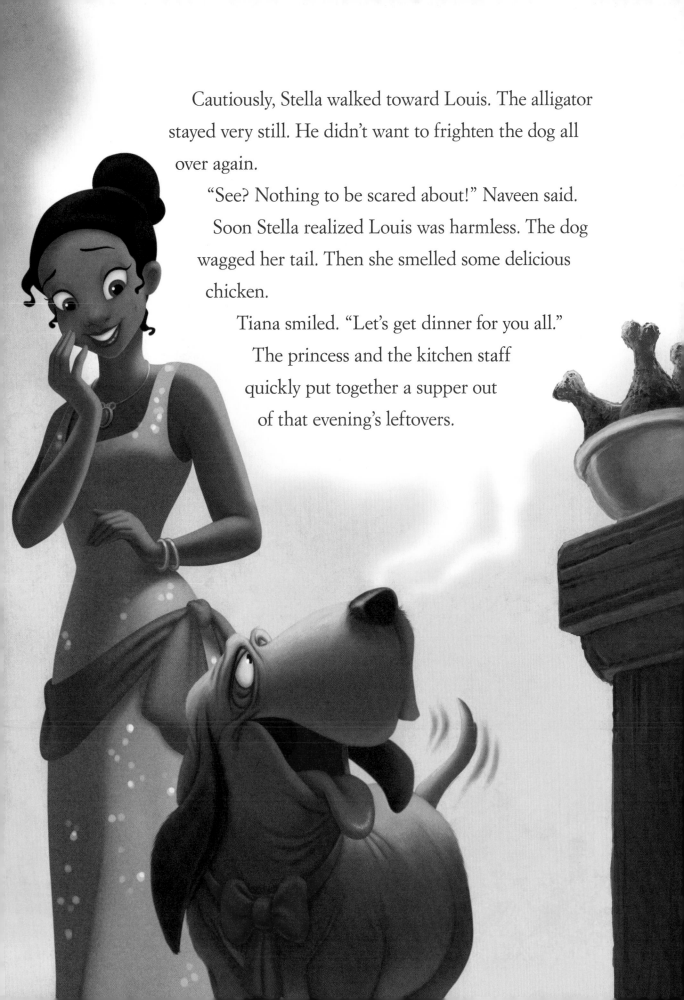

Cautiously, Stella walked toward Louis. The alligator stayed very still. He didn't want to frighten the dog all over again.

"See? Nothing to be scared about!" Naveen said.

Soon Stella realized Louis was harmless. The dog wagged her tail. Then she smelled some delicious chicken.

Tiana smiled. "Let's get dinner for you all." The princess and the kitchen staff quickly put together a supper out of that evening's leftovers.

Everyone went into the dining room. The staff ate while
Prince Naveen played the ukulele. Louis picked up his
trumpet and joined in the song. Some of the waiters and
waitresses began to dance. Stella didn't pay much attention,
though. She was eating some of Tiana's beignets.

A while later, the staff headed home. Tomorrow would
be another busy day at Tiana's Palace.

"Come along, Stella," Tiana told the dog. "Time for you
to go, too."

The prince and princess brought Stella to Charlotte's house. No one had noticed she was missing yet!

"Good night, Stella," Princess Tiana said, giving the dog a big hug. "Now that you know how much fun we have at the restaurant, you should come by more often."

Woof! Woof! Stella barked. She hadn't expected to have such an adventure that night. She knew she'd return to Tiana's Palace the next chance she got.

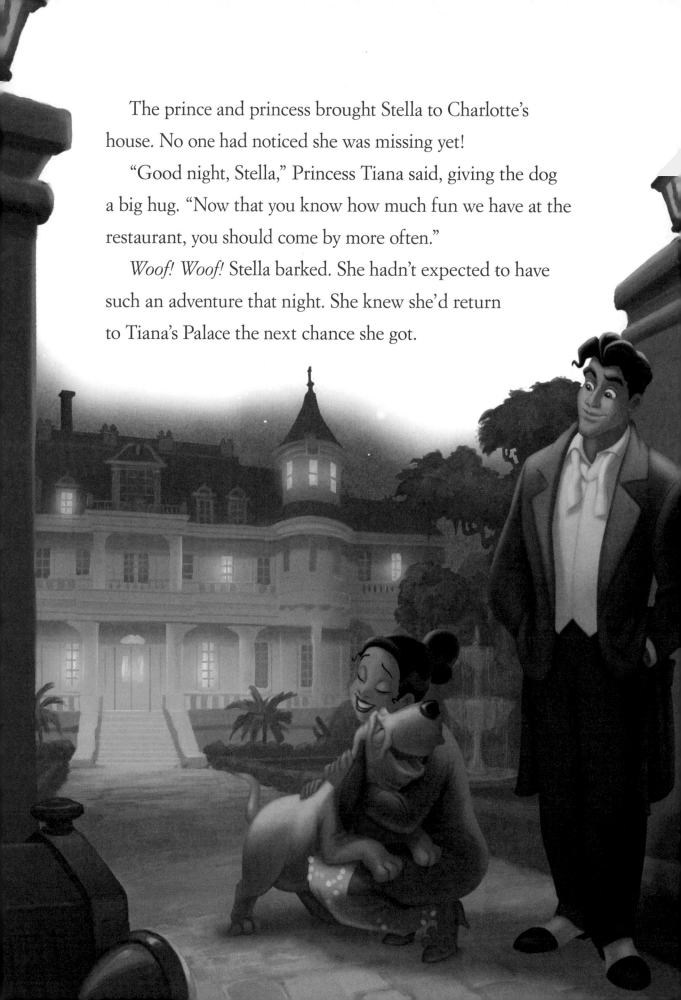

Aladdin
The Desert Race

Jasmine and Aladdin were strolling across the palace grounds one evening when the Sultan ran out onto the balcony.

"Drat!" the Sultan cried. "Oh, drat, drat, drat—that dratted Desert Race!"

Jasmine was surprised. Usually her father loved the Desert Race! Every year, the best riders from Agrabah competed against those of the neighboring kingdom of Zagrabah. The fastest horse and rider were awarded the prized Golden Palm trophy.

"What's the matter, Father?" Jasmine asked.

The Sultan shook his head sadly. "I just heard that Prince Fayiz will be riding for Zagrabah again. His horse is so fast he's won the race the last three years in a row!"

"I have an idea, Father!" Jasmine said eagerly. "I could ride Midnight in the Desert Race this year. He's the fastest horse in Agrabah!"

"Oh, dear me, no!" The Sultan looked shocked at the very suggestion. "The Desert Race can be dangerous. I won't have my daughter risking her neck like that!"

"How about if I ride Midnight in the race?" Aladdin spoke up.

The Sultan's face brightened immediately. "What a splendid idea!" he cried. "You'll have such fun, my boy!"

The next day, Aladdin and Jasmine went to the stables.

As soon as Aladdin was on Midnight, the horse threw him. Nobody but Jasmine had ever ridden him.

"Let me help," said the princess. Midnight gave her no trouble—as usual. The horse was ready to go.

Aladdin swung onto Midnight's back, but the horse still didn't want to cooperate. He kicked up his heels and sent Aladdin flying!

Aladdin brushed himself off.

"Here, let me try," Jasmine said. She easily climbed into the saddle. Midnight happily carried her around the stable yard, doing everything she asked.

"Sorry," Jasmine told Aladdin. "I guess Midnight is a one-person horse."

"Now how are we supposed to win that trophy back?" the Sultan asked.

"Let me ride in the race, Father," Jasmine urged.

The Sultan didn't seem to hear her. "Perhaps we can find Aladdin another fast horse." He didn't look hopeful, though.

"Don't worry," Aladdin said. "I'll think of something. . . ."

The day of the race arrived. Riders from Zagrabah paraded into Agrabah. Fayiz rode in on his impressive white stallion, Desert Warrior.

"I don't know why we bothered to bring the Golden Palm trophy," Fayiz announced haughtily. "We'll only have to carry it back to Zagrabah later."

Fans from both kingdoms gathered to watch the race. Soon the riders took their places at the starting line.

The Sultan looked at Aladdin. "What an odd-looking horse that boy is riding. I wonder why I've never seen it before." But he didn't have time to worry about that. "Now, where is Jasmine?" he wondered. "It's time to start the race!" The princess was nowhere to be found.

"We can't wait any longer, I suppose." The Sultan raised a flag to signal the start of the race. "One, two . . . three! And they're off!"

The riders galloped into the desert.

A black horse with a mysterious veiled rider took the lead right away. As soon as they were out of view of the palace, the rider threw off the veil. It was Jasmine!

"I do hate going against Father's wishes," she whispered to Midnight. "But I just had to prove that you were the fastest."

Aladdin was curious about the rider on the black horse. "Jasmine!" He gasped when he saw her.

Just then, his horse spotted the cool, inviting water of an oasis.

"Now that's more like it!" exclaimed the horse. Except the horse was actually the Genie! He jumped into the water and took the shape of a sea horse.

"Hey! This wasn't part of the plan!" Aladdin cried.

"Don't worry, Al," the Genie said. "We'll catch up. Gotta stay hydrated, you know!"

On land, Jasmine and Midnight galloped off without a backward glance.

Fayiz and Desert Warrior were starting to catch up. They were shocked when they saw the princess. Fayiz didn't want to lose to her.

Jasmine urged Midnight on, but the other horse was very fast. Finally, Desert Warrior pulled ahead.

"Give up now!" Fayiz shouted. "That trophy will always belong to Zagrabah!"

But Midnight wasn't finished yet. He surged forward again . . . and passed Desert Warrior!

"Not so fast!" Jasmine called to Fayiz with a laugh. "That trophy is in Agrabah, and that's where it is going to stay!"

Fayiz and Warrior stayed on Midnight's heels . . . until the horses had to jump a ditch that crossed the path. Midnight sailed over easily, but Warrior skidded to a stop!

With the other team out of the running, it seemed there was nothing to keep Jasmine and Midnight from winning. But then the princess heard the sound of hoofbeats close behind her.

"What?" she cried, looking back.

It was Aladdin! Jasmine hadn't even known he was still in the race!

Soon Aladdin and his mystery horse had caught up, and he and Jasmine were fighting for the lead. Jasmine was glad that the trophy would stay in Agrabah no matter which one of them won. But she really wanted to prove that Midnight was the fastest horse in the two kingdoms. She urged him on.

The two horses were neck and neck as they neared the finish line. First Midnight pulled ahead a tiny bit, then Aladdin's horse did. But neither could keep the lead. . . .

And so, the two horses crossed the finish line at the same time.

As soon as Midnight slowed to a stop, Jasmine jumped off, gave her tired horse a hug, and led him to the water trough. Then she walked over to Aladdin.

"Congratulations!" he said.

"Same to you," Jasmine replied. "But where in the world did you find such a fast horse?"

"Er . . ." Aladdin looked at his horse. Then he looked at
his feet. "Um, that is . . ." He didn't seem to know what to say.

"Surprise!" the Genie cried, transforming back into his
usual form.

Jasmine gasped. "Genie? That was *you*?"

"Sorry, Princess," the Genie said, winking. "We were just
horsing around."

Aladdin grinned sheepishly. "It was my idea. I couldn't
bear the thought of Zagrabah winning again this year."

"Oh, dear," the Sultan said. "The rules state that it must be a horse-and-rider team—not a *genie*-and-rider team! I'm afraid this disqualifies you two from the race." Then he smiled. "And that means Jasmine and Midnight are the winners!"

Jasmine changed into a new outfit. At the award ceremony, she patted Midnight. Jasmine had always known her horse was fast, but she'd never imagined he could beat a genie!

Snow White
and the Seven Dwarfs

A Big Surprise

Snow White and her prince had recently been married, and they were living happily at the castle. The Seven Dwarfs missed Snow White, but she made sure to visit them often.

One spring day, Snow White went to the Dwarfs' cottage. The Dwarfs were not expecting her, but the princess had a very special surprise planned for them.

Snow White knew the Dwarfs worked hard. That day,
she wanted to make sure that when they got home, they
didn't have to do any more work—no dusting, no sweeping,
and no cooking.

Snow White waited until the Dwarfs had left. Then
she and her animal friends hurried into the cottage.
The princess looked around. "By the time the
Dwarfs get home tonight, our surprise will be ready."

So they set to work. Snow White sang a cheerful song
as she swept the cottage floor. The birds chirped while they
picked up crumbs. The squirrels used their fluffy tails to dust.
And the chipmunks and deer washed and dried the breakfast
dishes. With so many helpers, Snow White had the downstairs
gleaming in no time.

Next, they went upstairs, and the princess began to make the beds.

"Pull the covers up tight," she told the bunnies. "Then fold down the top. There, it's perfect!"

The bunnies hopped off to start on the other beds.

Before long, every inch of the Dwarfs' cottage was neat and tidy. Snow White and the animals headed outside to gather fresh berries, nuts, and apples to use in the Dwarfs' supper.

"They'll be very hungry after their long day," said the princess. Luckily, the blueberry bushes had lots of ripe fruit, and the basket was quickly filled. "I know what we'll make for dessert," Snow White told the rabbits. "Blueberry pie!"

Next, the princess and her friends strolled into a meadow to find some wildflowers.

"Lovely!" said Snow White as she sniffed a blossom. "These will be perfect for the table."

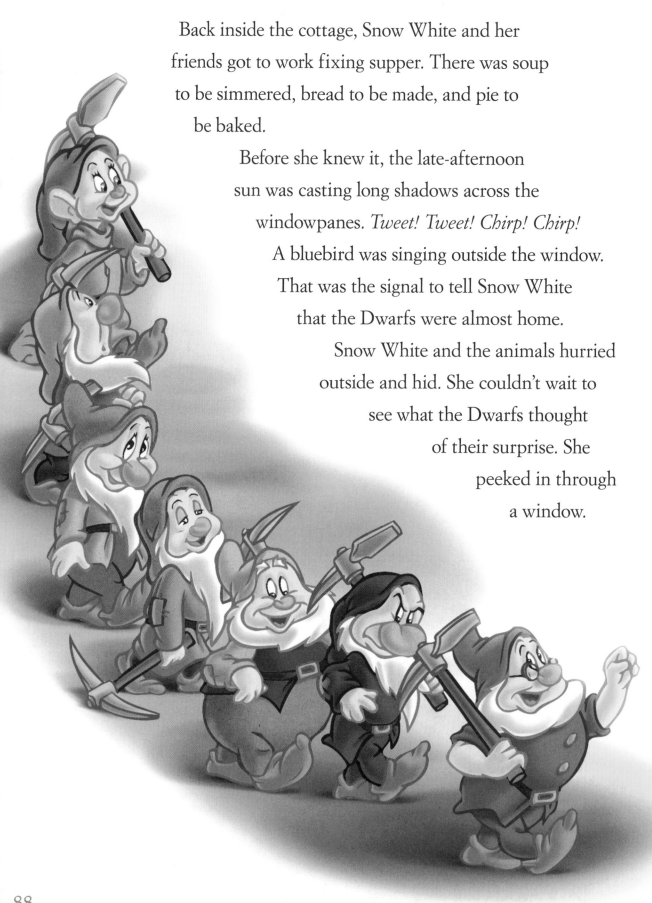

Back inside the cottage, Snow White and her
friends got to work fixing supper. There was soup
to be simmered, bread to be made, and pie to
be baked.

Before she knew it, the late-afternoon
sun was casting long shadows across the
windowpanes. *Tweet! Tweet! Chirp! Chirp!*
A bluebird was singing outside the window.
That was the signal to tell Snow White
that the Dwarfs were almost home.

Snow White and the animals hurried
outside and hid. She couldn't wait to
see what the Dwarfs thought
of their surprise. She
peeked in through
a window.

When they got inside, the Dwarfs stopped and stared.
They could not believe their eyes. The floors were swept,
the room was tidy, and there was even a freshly baked pie
cooling on a windowsill!

"What is that delicious smell?" Doc wondered.

"Look!" cried Grumpy. He pointed to the table,
which had been set. Then he went to the pot of soup.
"Someone's been in our house."

The Dwarfs were confused. They tried to guess which Dwarf had done all of this.

Doc noticed that Happy's smile was especially big. Was he keeping a secret? Dopey pointed out that Sneezy seemed supersneezy. Maybe because he had dusted and swept the cottage?

Snow White giggled as she listened outside the window. "They'll never guess that we did it," she whispered to her animal friends.

When the Dwarfs started to eat their pie, Snow White quietly headed home.

Inside the cottage, Bashful had one more guess. Whoever was behind the surprise would have to be one tired Dwarf! And who seemed the sleepiest? Why, Sleepy, of course!

The truth was, Sleepy wasn't the only one. After a long workday, their tummies pleasantly full, all Seven Dwarfs were ready for bed.

When they climbed the stairs, the Dwarfs found one last treat: seven neatly made beds and seven perfectly fluffed pillows. As they drifted off to sleep, the Dwarfs decided to tell their good friend Snow White about this wonderful surprise the very next time they saw her.

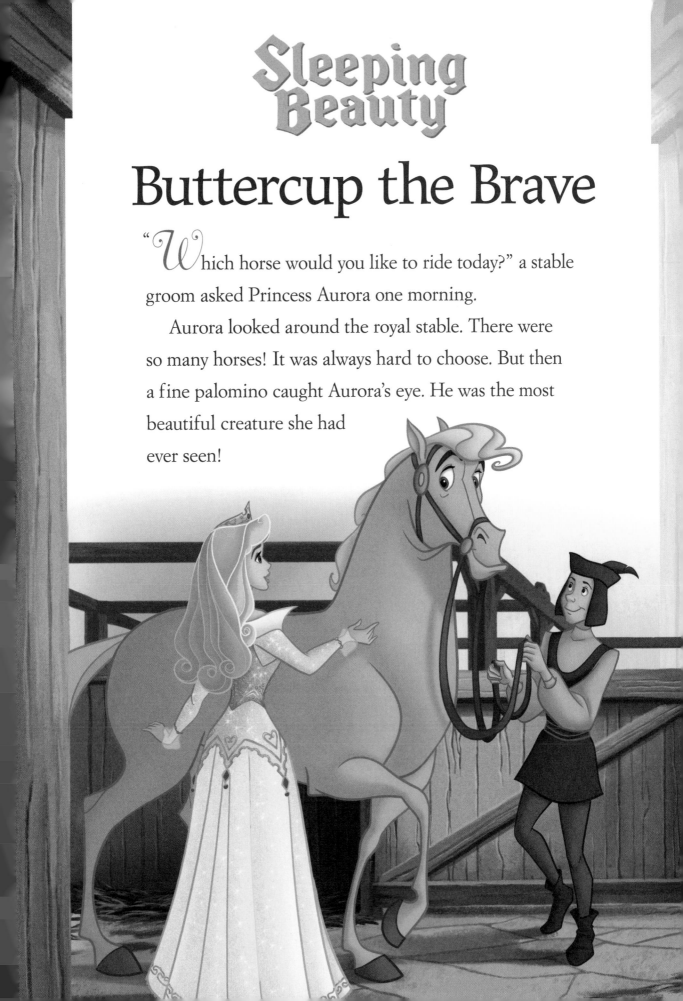

Sleeping Beauty

Buttercup the Brave

"Which horse would you like to ride today?" a stable groom asked Princess Aurora one morning.

Aurora looked around the royal stable. There were so many horses! It was always hard to choose. But then a fine palomino caught Aurora's eye. He was the most beautiful creature she had ever seen!

Aurora rode the former warhorse around the palace courtyard. The horse marched as confidently as if he were the king himself.

Suddenly the princess had an idea. "From now on, I think I'd like to ride the same horse every day," she said.

"What a wonderful idea," Prince Phillip agreed. "You should have a horse of your own."

"What's this horse's name?" Aurora asked.

"We call him Brutus, Your Highness," the groom replied.

"Oh, no!" Aurora exclaimed. "That won't do at all. I think I'll call him . . . Buttercup."

Phillip and the groom looked surprised. "Er—are you sure?" the prince asked.

Aurora smiled. "Do *you* like your new name, Buttercup?"

The horse snorted happily.

Aurora rode Buttercup around the castle grounds. When the pages blew their trumpets as they rode by, he didn't flinch. When a carriage rumbled past, he stood at attention. When Aurora asked him to jump over a stone wall, he cleared it effortlessly.

The next day, Aurora decided to ride Buttercup out to the fairies' cottage.

"Why don't you let me saddle up Samson and come with you?" Phillip suggested, looking worried.

"Don't be silly," Aurora said with a laugh. "I grew up in those woods, remember? Besides, I'll be with Buttercup. He'll take care of me!"

Aurora and Buttercup pranced off. But the moment they entered the woods, Buttercup became a different horse.

He began to walk slowly and look around nervously. When some of Aurora's woodland friends appeared, Buttercup tried to run away!

"What's the matter, Buttercup?" Aurora asked. "Why, there's nothing to be frightened of!"

She could hardly believe the change in her horse. He was even afraid to step over a branch.

When she asked him to walk through a forest stream, he nearly fainted!

By the time she reached the cottage, Aurora was feeling a bit frustrated. How could a horse who was so brave at the palace be so timid in the woods?

Flora, Fauna, and Merryweather hurried out of their cottage.

"Oh, what a beautiful pony!" Merryweather exclaimed.

Aurora sighed. "He is beautiful," she said. "But he seems to be afraid of everything in the woods!"

"I'm sure it will be all right," Flora said. "You'll just need to be patient with him, that's all."

"Yes, dear, be patient," Merryweather agreed. But she sounded distracted. She moved closer to the horse. "What a nice coat he has!"

"And such shiny hooves," Fauna added.

"Though he might look even nicer if his hooves were another color," Merryweather mused. *Zap!* She aimed her wand. Just like that, Buttercup's hooves turned blue!

"Oh, don't be silly!" Flora exclaimed. "A horse shouldn't have blue hooves. On the other hand, he might look pretty in pink. . . ."

Zap! Buttercup's hooves returned to their normal color. But the rest of him turned pink.

"Quit that!" Merryweather cried. "Blue!"

"Pink!" Flora argued back.

Zap! Zap!

As the two fairies argued, the horse changed from one color to the next.

Aurora watched her new horse change color. That
didn't seem to bother him at all. But when a stray leaf
fluttered down, he jumped and snorted as if it were
a horse-eating dragon.

What was she going to do? She didn't want to give up
on him. Buttercup was so perfect in every other way.

Soon it was time to say good-bye to the fairies. Aurora did
her best to ignore the way Buttercup hesitated at every shadow
on the trail home. She had been certain that Buttercup was
the perfect horse for her. Now she wasn't so sure.

Suddenly, Buttercup stopped abruptly.

"What is it *this* time?" Aurora asked with a sigh.

Then she looked at the trail ahead . . . and gasped in horror. An enormous mountain lion was blocking their path!

Aurora's heart pounded as she watched the creature creep closer. If Buttercup could be scared by a bunny rabbit, he was certain to go crazy over a mountain lion.

They were in big trouble!

To Aurora's surprise, Buttercup didn't panic or try to run. Instead, he stood proudly and puffed himself up to look even bigger than he was. He planted his hooves and snorted angrily at the mountain lion.

Then he marched forward and struck out at the lion with his front hooves! Aurora hung on. She was still scared. But it seemed that Buttercup wasn't!

Buttercup's lack of fear made Aurora feel braver. She reached out and grabbed a sturdy tree branch.

"Leave us alone!" she yelled at the mountain lion, waving the branch. "Or else!"

Buttercup pawed at the ground and added a fierce snort to back up Aurora's words.

When the mountain lion didn't budge, Buttercup leaped forward and pinned its tail to the ground with one hoof. Then Aurora reached out and gave the lion a smart rap on the nose with her branch.

The lion let out an embarrassed yowl. Then it yanked its tail free and raced away.

Aurora was pleased with herself—and with her horse. Buttercup had been brave when it really counted.

"Come on, Buttercup," she said, giving him a pat. "Let's go home."

Buttercup snorted again, proudly, and pranced off.

As Aurora and Buttercup neared the castle, a butterfly fluttered past. Buttercup's eyes went wide, and he jumped in terror.

Aurora stroked Buttercup's neck and talked to him in a soft voice, reminding him to stay calm. The butterfly fluttered closer and closer . . . and finally landed right on his nose (which was only trembling a *little*).

"Good boy!" she praised him. "You know, Buttercup, I think we make a perfect team!"

Beauty and the Beast
A Friend for Philippe

*I*t was a beautiful morning when Belle arrived at Philippe's stable with a surprise for her friend. "Guess what I have!" she called happily as she hurried to the horse's stall. "The first carrots of the season, Philippe! I picked them just for you."

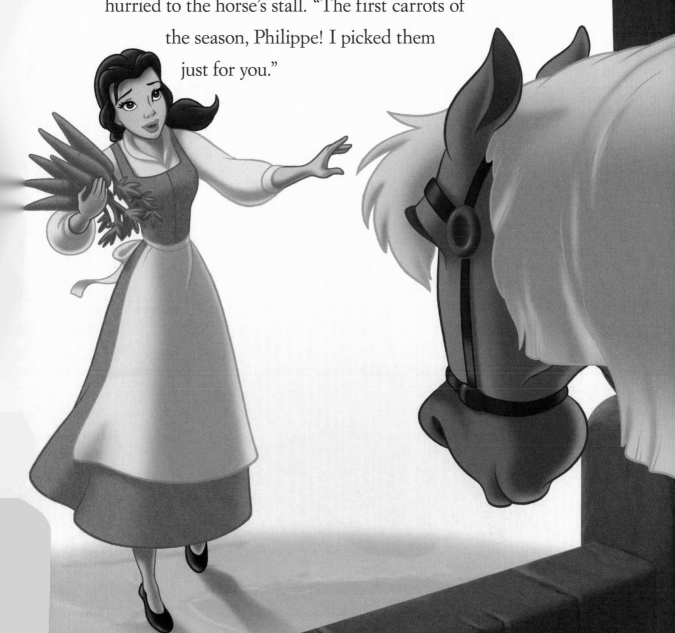

Philippe was not as happy as Belle had hoped. He sniffed at the bunch of carrots. But when Belle offered him one, the horse pushed her hand away.

"Is something wrong?" Belle asked, alarmed. Philippe was always hungry.

Philippe hung his head and sighed.

Belle decided that she had to cheer up her friend. But how?

"If only you could talk," Belle said, "you could tell me exactly what to do."

Later that morning, Belle hurried to the castle library. She gathered all the books about horses she could find and began to read.

"Sacre bleu!" cried Lumiere when he, Cogsworth, and Chip saw all the books. "What are you doing, Princess?"

"I want to cheer up Philippe," Belle explained. "I hoped these books would help me figure out what's wrong, but I'm not having much luck."

"You should brighten his stall!" Lumiere suggested. "It's important to have the right atmosphere, you know!"

"I believe that music is the key to happiness," Cogsworth said. "It always made me smile when I was an enchanted clock."

"Or how about a bubble bath?" Chip chimed in. "That used to cheer me up!"

Belle decided to give each idea a try.

First, she and Lumiere decorated Philippe's stall. They covered the walls with wallpaper and sprinkled flower petals on the floor. They piled pillows in the corners, hung curtains on the windows, and strung up beaded garlands. For a final touch, they hung a chandelier from the ceiling.

"*Voilà!*" Lumiere exclaimed. "What more could
a horse ask for?"

Philippe stared sadly out the window.

"I wish I knew," said Belle.

Next, Cogsworth brought an orchestra to the stable. Belle, Lumiere, and Chip listened politely as Cogsworth led the musicians through a very long concert.

Philippe didn't seem to enjoy the music, though.

Finally, Belle saw to it that Philippe was treated to a bubble bath fit for a king.

"If this doesn't make him smile," Belle told Chip, "I don't know what will!"

In the end, although he was shiny and sweet-smelling, Philippe was still glum—and Belle was still puzzled.

"Maybe the Prince will know what to do," Chip suggested.

Belle thought that was an excellent idea. She found the Prince in his study and explained everything to him. "I wish I knew what Philippe needed!" she cried. "Do you have any suggestions?"

The Prince thought for a moment. "Maybe a walk would do him good," he said. "That always used to cheer me up."

"Of course!" Belle agreed. "That's a wonderful idea!"

Bright and early the next morning, Belle changed into her riding clothes and fetched Philippe. She led him to the edge of the forest where the royal orchards began. The sight of all of the delicious fruit gave Belle an idea.

"Would you like an apple?" the princess asked. "Go ahead and choose one!"

Philippe wandered from tree to tree, eyeing each apple and even sniffing some. But he looked sad, and his steps were slow and heavy. It was clear his heart wasn't in it.

They continued until they reached a meadow.

All of a sudden, Philippe's ears pricked up, and his head snapped to attention. Then he charged off like a racehorse.

"Whoa, boy!" Belle cried, nearly falling out of the saddle. "Where are you going?"

But Philippe galloped on, straight into the forest.

At last they emerged . . . into a clearing filled with wild horses! Philippe whinnied, and several of the horses answered him.

Finally, Belle realized what Philippe had wanted.
Not a fancy stall or fine music or a bubble bath.

He wanted to be with other horses!

Philippe trotted eagerly over to the herd.

"Well, go on," Belle said as she swung out of the
saddle. "Go have some fun!"

Soon Philippe was playing with one of the horses.

The two horses chased each other around the
clearing and found a patch of delicious grass.

All too quickly, the day was over, and the sun began to set.

"Oh, goodness! We've got to get going! I promise we'll come back soon," Belle told Philippe.

As they started toward the castle, Belle heard the sound of hooves behind them.

"Well, look at that, Philippe!" she exclaimed. "It's your new friend."

The horse who had played with Philippe all afternoon was following them home! By the time they reached the castle, the two horses were walking side by side.

"Welcome to our castle!" Belle told the new horse when they arrived. "We're honored to have you as our guest!"

To show the horse she meant it, Belle fixed up the stall next to Philippe's.

"There," she said when she was through. "Now this looks like a stable where a horse—or two—could live happily ever after!"

And that is exactly what they did.

Cinderella
A Royal Friend

"The princess is coming!" a crowd of girls exclaimed as they watched Cinderella's coach approach their school.

"Let me see!" cried Emma, who had arrived at the school only a few days earlier. "I want to see the princess!"

"Don't worry, you will," replied Claire, who was the oldest. "She's coming to visit us."

Sure enough, the coach came to a stop right outside.

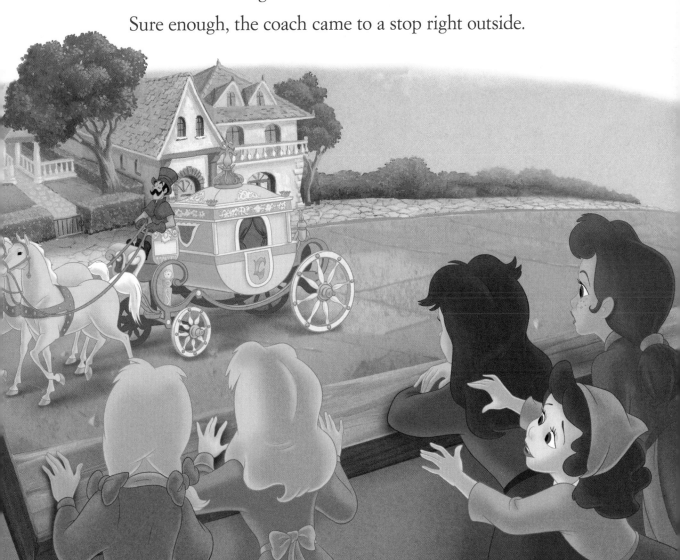

A royal trumpeter blew his horn loudly to announce Cinderella's arrival.

"Quickly, girls, gather around," said the headmistress of the school. She hurried to open the door. "Welcome, Your Highness!" she exclaimed. She and the girls curtsied as Cinderella entered the room.

"It's so nice to see you all again," said the princess.

Cinderella liked to stop by the school to help the girls with their reading and writing.

She also brought books, clothes, toys, and food. Many of the girls were poor and had few things of their own. Everyone was happy to see Cinderella. But no one was more excited than Emma.

Cinderella and the girls spent a wonderful afternoon together.

After their lessons, they sang, danced, and told stories. Then they read together and played with some of the toys the princess had brought.

When it was time for Cinderella to go, she made an announcement. "In one week, there will be a party at the castle—to be held in your honor."

"For us?" the girls shouted excitedly.

"But what will we wear?" asked Emma.

Cinderella smiled. "Why, the dresses I am having made for each of you, of course! And you shall have new shoes and gloves as well! I remember how much fun it was when I got to dress up for a ball the first time. I thought all of you would like to wear fancy gowns, too."

The next day, the girls talked about nothing but the party. They couldn't wait to dress up.

To distract them, the headmistress decided they should go outside. "It's a lovely day," she announced. "Let's have a picnic."

The girls climbed a hill and spread blankets in the meadow near the royal estate. While her classmates ran and played, Emma gazed at the castle. She couldn't wait to see what it looked like inside. She thought it must be the most wonderful place in the whole world.

Soon, Emma noticed a group of seamstresses walking toward the castle gates. She ran over to them.

A guard opened the gates for the seamstresses. Without thinking, Emma slipped behind them and walked straight into the castle! Then she ducked behind a curtain.

Cinderella welcomed the women, then led them up a staircase. When everyone was gone, Emma ran up the stairs and began to explore.

In one room, Emma found a huge bed with a pink, ruffled canopy. She climbed into it and closed her eyes for a moment.

Cinderella's mouse friends Jaq, Gus, and Mary came out from under the bed and introduced themselves.

Suddenly, they heard someone down the hall say, "This fabric is gorgeous!"

Emma and the mice ran toward the voice and found a room filled with seamstresses. They were busy cutting satin, silk, and velvet.

"Come in! Come in!" a seamstress called. "Stand here, dear. Now, hold still." The woman began draping fabric around Emma. She thought Cinderella had sent her to model the dresses.

Emma just smiled. She loved the swishing sound the cloth made. She also loved the way everyone fussed over her.

When Cinderella stopped by a while later, Emma was wearing one of the dresses.

"More bows, please," Emma requested. "And another layer of ruffles."

"Oh, my!" exclaimed Cinderella. "That certainly is a fancy dress! And you look beautiful in it."

Cinderella thought the seamstresses had brought Emma. The princess remembered what it was like to do chores all day. So she invited Emma to have tea with her.

They sat at a table laid with delicate china and gleaming silver. A servant brought in tea and cakes and cookies.

"It must be wonderful to be a princess," Emma said between bites. "You get to wear fancy clothes, go to parties all day, and order servants around."

Cinderella laughed. "When a princess wants something, she asks politely. And there's much more to being a princess than clothes and parties," she replied. "Why don't you help me this afternoon and see what a princess *really* does?"

For the next few hours, Emma and Cinderella put together baskets of food, clothing, books, and toys. Emma's favorite part was going through Cinderella's wardrobe to look for old clothes that could be donated.

Soon, it was time to deliver the baskets to the schools and orphanages. As they passed through the village in the royal carriage, Emma waved at a passerby. Princess Emma, she thought. I like the sound of that!

When they arrived at her school, the headmistress gave Emma a big hug. "Where have you been?" she cried. "We've been so worried."

The headmistress and the other girls had been looking for Emma all afternoon.

"But I thought the seamstresses brought you to work," Cinderella said, puzzled.

Emma explained how she'd snuck into the castle. "I'm sorry," she said. "I didn't mean to make anyone worry. I just wanted to see what being a princess was like."

"Being a princess is more than just playing dress-up," Cinderella told her. "It also means being responsible."

"Why don't you come to the castle each day?" Cinderella suggested. "Then you can learn more about what princesses really do."

Every afternoon when Emma's lessons were over, she went to the castle. The princess was always very busy. She oversaw the castle staff. She visited the shopkeepers and farmers to make sure everything was running smoothly. She even got the court jester to tell jokes to children who were ill.

Emma tagged along everywhere. Cinderella decided she should help plan the party for the girls' school.

So Emma helped to decorate. She also helped the cook make a cake.

Cinderella was so impressed that she asked her mouse friends to make a special dress for Emma.

"It's fit for a princess!" Emma exclaimed when she saw it.

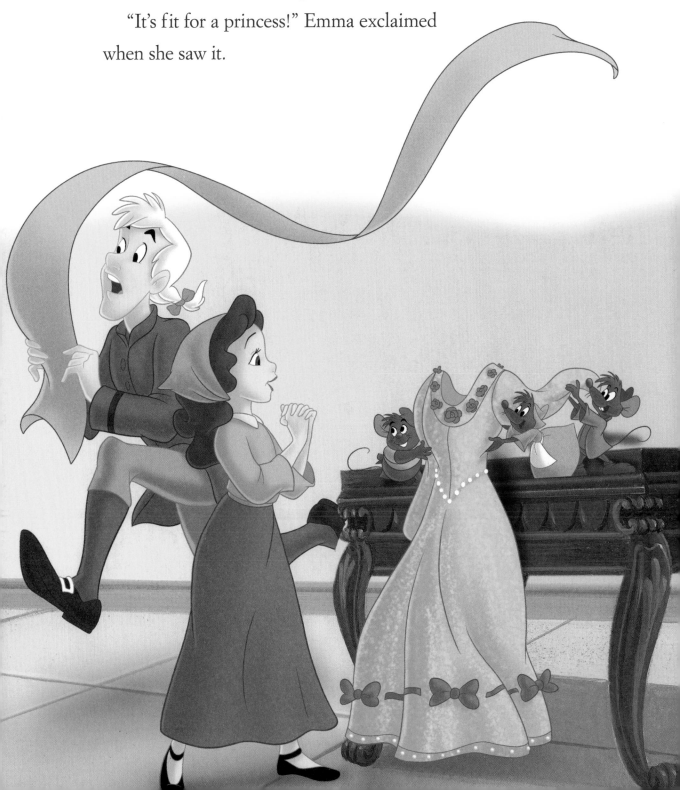

Finally, the night of the party arrived. The girls twirled around the dance floor in magnificent new dresses.

"I still wish I could be a real princess," said Emma.

"Because you've worked so hard, I'm going to make you an honorary princess for the evening," Cinderella said with a smile.

"Oh, thank you!" the girl cried happily. She was thrilled that she'd get to be Princess Emma for one magical night.

Tangled

Rapunzel's Story

Once upon a time, there was a magical kingdom ruled by a good queen and a kind king. They were happy until the Queen became very sick.

The King had heard of a flower with healing powers and sent his guards to dig it up. Unfortunately, the flower belonged to a wicked woman named Mother Gothel.

Losing the flower made Mother Gothel furious. So when the King and Queen had a baby, she stole the child away!

Mother Gothel hid the girl, Rapunzel, in a secret tower for almost eighteen years. It turned out that Rapunzel's hair, which was magnificently long, had the same healing powers as the flower. Mother Gothel used it to keep herself young and never told the girl she wasn't really her mother.

The Queen and King never forgot their lost princess. Each year, on her birthday, they sent lanterns floating through the night sky.

Rapunzel didn't know that the floating lights she saw from her window were lanterns. But her dearest wish was to see the lights up close. "Not just from my window," she said.

But Mother Gothel wouldn't let her go. She needed Rapunzel's magic in order to stay young. Instead, she told Rapunzel that the world outside was a scary place, too dangerous for her. "Trust me, pet," she said. "Mother knows best."

One day Mother Gothel went away. Before long,
someone climbed the tower. He slipped through the
window and—*BANG!* Rapunzel knocked him out with
a frying pan.

The man, Flynn Rider, was a thief on the run from
the palace guards. Rapunzel searched his bag. Inside
was a stolen crown. She tried it on.

Rapunzel knew this was her only chance to see the floating lights. Flynn could be her guide outside the tower! When Flynn woke up, she offered him a deal.

"Deal?" Flynn asked. He was still dazed from the frying pan.

Rapunzel showed him a painting of the lights. "Take me to these," she said.

Flynn shook his head. "No can do." He did not want to go to the city. He was trying to hide from the Stabbington brothers, two thieves he had been in business with. The palace guards were also still chasing Flynn.

But Rapunzel had a bargaining chip—the crown. She'd return it only if Flynn helped her.

So Flynn reluctantly climbed down the tower, and Rapunzel used her hair to lower herself to the ground.

The outside world was like a dream come true to her. She'd never run through grass before, or climbed a tree, or sat in a field of flowers. Still, she felt nervous. Mother Gothel had said the outside world was scary. And Mother Gothel wouldn't lie . . . would she?

Flynn tried to frighten Rapunzel into going home. He
took her to the scariest place he knew—the Snuggly Duckling.
It was a tavern full of thugs!

The thugs glared at Rapunzel, but when she sang about
her dream of seeing the lanterns, they all became friends. The
men even showed Rapunzel and Flynn a secret passage out of
the tavern . . . just in time, too. The palace guards had tracked
down Flynn and his stolen crown.

As they were escaping, Flynn hurt his hand on a sharp rock. That night, Rapunzel wrapped her hair around it, and his hand was healed!

Flynn was amazed, so Rapunzel explained about her magical hair. "But once it's cut," she said, "it loses its power."

They sat close together by the campfire. Flynn was starting to fall for Rapunzel. And Rapunzel liked Flynn a lot, too. But could she trust him?

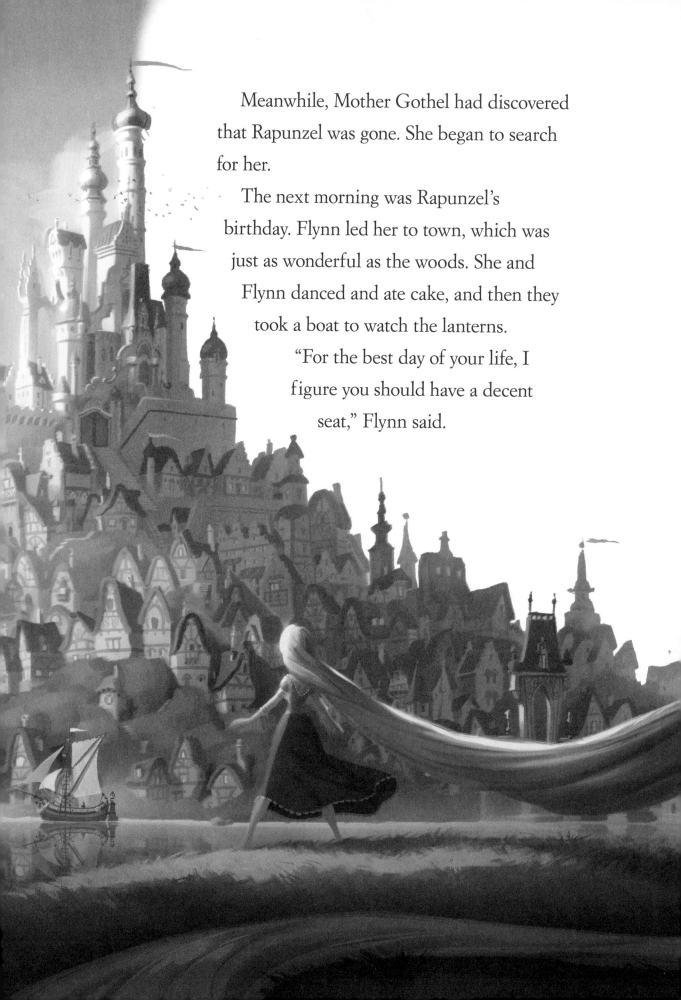

Meanwhile, Mother Gothel had discovered that Rapunzel was gone. She began to search for her.

The next morning was Rapunzel's birthday. Flynn led her to town, which was just as wonderful as the woods. She and Flynn danced and ate cake, and then they took a boat to watch the lanterns.

"For the best day of your life, I figure you should have a decent seat," Flynn said.

Twilight came, and glowing lanterns filled the sky. Rapunzel was so excited to see the lights that she almost tipped the boat over.

"I have something for you, too," she told Flynn. She handed him the crown. She finally trusted him.

Flynn knew what he had to do.

Flynn went ashore and tried to give the crown to the
Stabbington brothers—but the thieves knocked him out. Then
they found Rapunzel and convinced her that Flynn had given
her up.

"A fair trade," they said. "A crown for the girl with the
magic hair."

"No!" Rapunzel cried. She tried to run away, but she
couldn't.

THUMP! CRASH! Mother Gothel rushed in. She rescued
Rapunzel from the thieves! She didn't tell Rapunzel she'd told
the brothers to try to capture her in the first place.

Mother Gothel and Rapunzel returned to the tower. But Rapunzel couldn't stop thinking of everything she'd seen. Suddenly, all the pieces fell into place. "I'm the lost princess," she realized.

Mother Gothel froze.

"It was you!" Rapunzel said bitterly. "I should have been hiding from you."

Instantly, Mother Gothel stopped pretending to be nice. She tied up Rapunzel. Soon Flynn came to the tower, looking for Rapunzel. Mother Gothel hurt him.

Rapunzel knew she could heal Flynn with her hair. "I'll stay with you," she promised Mother Gothel. "Just let me save him."

"Swear it," Mother Gothel said. And Rapunzel did.

Flynn refused to let Mother Gothel win. Grabbing a shard from a broken mirror, he sliced off Rapunzel's hair. Immediately, it turned brown.

"What have you done?" Mother Gothel shrieked. As Rapunzel's hair lost its power, Mother Gothel became very, very old. Soon she was gone.

Rapunzel held Flynn tight. Without her hair, she couldn't heal him. He slipped away.

A single tear fell from her face. It landed on Flynn and began to glow. His eyes opened. The magic in her tear had saved him!

Overjoyed, Rapunzel and Flynn soon went to the palace.

Rapunzel was welcomed by the King and Queen, her real mother and father. They couldn't have been happier to have their daughter back. She wasn't the baby they'd lost anymore, but she was a lovely princess.

And although Rapunzel's hair was no longer magical, she was still the most enchanting girl Flynn had ever met.

Sleeping Beauty

Aurora and the Helpful Dragon

"I'll race you to the lookout point!" Princess Aurora called to Prince Phillip as they galloped through the forest one sunny morning. She sped away on her horse, Buttercup, with Prince Phillip close behind.

As they rounded a bend, a small dragon popped out from behind a tree.

The prince and princess went to it at once.

"*Grrgrrgrr?*" the little dragon said softly.

"Oh, he's so cute!" Aurora exclaimed.

Phillip was worried. "Dragons can be dangerous!"

The little dragon shook his head.

Aurora laughed. "I think he's saying he's not dangerous. Let's take him home. I'm going to call him Crackle!"

"He does seem like a harmless little fellow," Phillip agreed.

Aurora picked up Crackle, but Buttercup was afraid. He tossed his mane and pawed the ground. Then Crackle licked the horse's nose! Buttercup blinked with surprise and nuzzled Crackle's cheek. The little dragon giggled.

"Buttercup likes Crackle!" Aurora exclaimed.

When Phillip and Aurora rode into the courtyard, the three good fairies were hanging banners for a ball. King Stefan and his wife were coming to visit.

Flora gasped when she saw Crackle. "Dragons can be dangerous."

"Remember the last one!" Fauna added.

"Oooh, I think he's sweet," Merryweather spoke up.

"Grrrgrr," Crackle babbled.

"He seems to think you're sweet, too," Aurora told Merryweather.

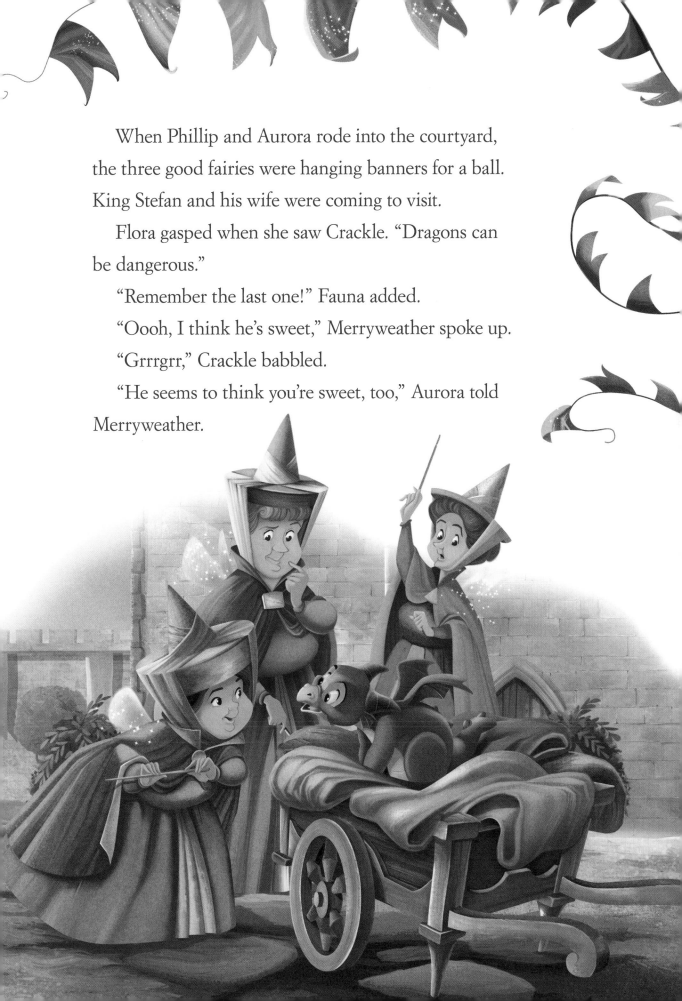

Just then, Crackle noticed a kitten in a basket of yarn.

Crackle listened to it purring. Then he scrunched up his mouth and closed his eyes. He tried to purr. *"Purrgrr, purrgrr!"* Clouds of smoke streamed from his nose and mouth.

"Aachoo! Aachoo! Ah-ah-ah-CHOO!" The fairies sneezed so hard from the smoke that they tumbled backward!

Crackle looked sad for a moment. Then he saw the kitten playing with a ball of yarn, and he snatched some. *Whoosh!* The yarn burst into flames! Merryweather put out the fire with her wand.

"Oh, Crackle," Aurora said gently. "You're not a kitten. You're a dragon."

Crackle's lower lip trembled.

A moment later, Phillip led the horses into the stable.
A dog followed, barking and wagging his tail. Crackle ran
after them, wagging his tail, too.

He tried to bark. *"Woofgrr, woofgrr."*
Flames shot from his mouth, and
some straw caught fire.

Phillip poured water on
the burning straw.

"You're not a dog,"
he said kindly, shooing
Crackle away.

Sadly, the little
dragon crept out
of the stable.

Aurora noticed that Crackle looked unhappy, so she took
him to the castle. As the princess began to tell a story, a bird
sang by the window.

Crackle's ears perked up. He tried to sing like a bird.

"LAAAlaagrr!" he bellowed.

King Hubert heard the racket and rushed into the room.

"Oh, my, my, my! How did a dragon get in here?" he
shouted.

Crackle had never heard a loud, angry voice before.
Frightened, he ran to the garden.

Aurora chased after Crackle. At last, she found the little dragon sitting beside a fountain, watching a fish.

Splash! Before Aurora could stop him, Crackle jumped into the water.

"Crackle, you're not a fish!" Aurora exclaimed as she pulled the dragon from the pool. "You're not a kitten, or a dog, or a bird either. You're a dragon!"

Tears rolled down Crackle's face. *"Grrgrrgrr,"* he sobbed.

Suddenly, Aurora understood.

"Do you think no one will like you because you're a dragon?" she asked.

Crackle nodded and whimpered.

"You can't change what you are," Aurora said kindly. "But you don't have to be dangerous. You can be a helpful dragon."

Crackle stopped crying. *"Grrgrrgrrgrr?"* he murmured hopefully.

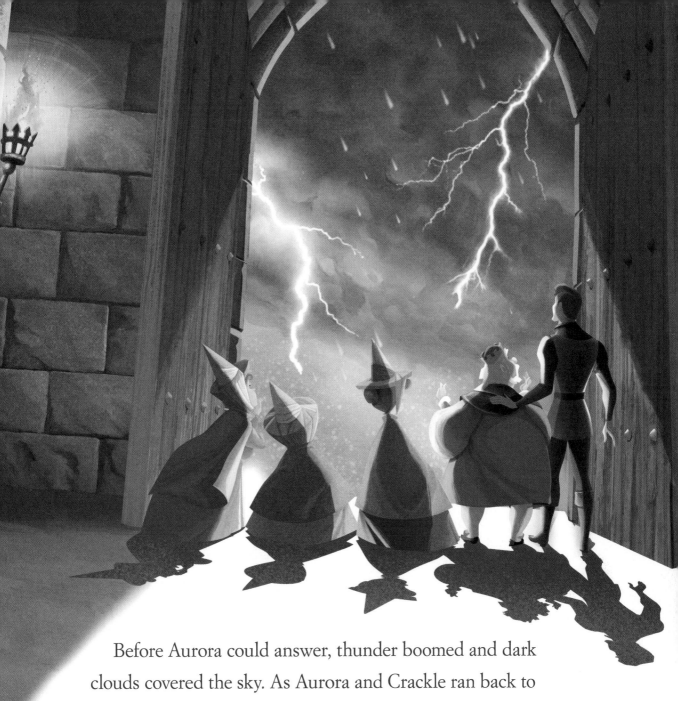

Before Aurora could answer, thunder boomed and dark clouds covered the sky. As Aurora and Crackle ran back to the castle, rain began to pour down. Everyone was gathered in the grand hallway, watching the storm.

"I'm afraid King Stefan and the queen might lose their way," Prince Phillip said, concerned.

Aurora looked at Crackle. "Do you want to show everyone that you're a kind, brave dragon?" she asked.

"GRRRgrrrgrr!" Crackle exclaimed enthusiastically.

"Fly to the top of the highest tower," Aurora instructed.
"Then blow the largest, brightest flames you can to help guide
my parents to the castle."

A moment later, the little dragon soared upward.

"Be careful!" the princess called.

Everyone tried to see Crackle, but it was too dark.

Suddenly, gold and red flames lit up the sky above the watchtower. Crackle had done it!

Again and again, Crackle blew his flames.

At last, Phillip shouted, "I see King Stefan's coach! They're almost here!"

Everyone hurried to greet the visitors.

"The tower light saved us!" King Stefan exclaimed. "I need one like it!"

At that moment Crackle flew into the hall.

"Well, there he is! Our new tower light," King Hubert said with a laugh.

"A dragon?" King Stefan asked. "But dragons are danger—"

"Not Crackle," Aurora interrupted. "He's a brave and helpful dragon!"

THE LITTLE MERMAID
Ariel to the Rescue

"Oh, Eric! This is wonderful!" Ariel said excitedly as she twirled around the ballroom with her prince. "I can dance with you *and* see the ocean!"

"Do you miss your sea friends?" he asked.

"Sometimes," Ariel replied a bit sadly. "But I love being with you."

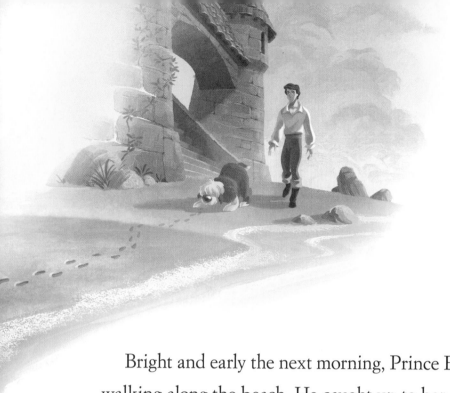

Bright and early the next morning, Prince Eric saw Ariel walking along the beach. He caught up to her, and they strolled together along the sand. The prince knew Ariel was hoping to visit Flounder and Sebastian, as well as her other friends from the sea. But they were nowhere to be found.

Eric and Ariel watched the waves crash onto the shore.

"It's rough out there today. If I were a fish, I think I might be too scared to come close to shore," the prince said gently. "Don't worry, Ariel. We'll figure out a way to bring together the land and the sea."

At dusk, Ariel went to Eric.
"I was thinking about what you said
earlier," she said. "I want to show you
something."

Ariel led the prince to the quiet lagoon
they had rowed in long ago.

"Do you think my friends would feel safer
visiting me here?" she asked.

Eric rubbed his chin. "*Hmmm.* Maybe."

He had an idea, but he wanted to make sure it
would work before he said anything to Ariel.

A few weeks later, Eric found Ariel walking along the beach again.

"Come with me," he said. "I have a surprise for you."

He took her to the lagoon. The first thing Ariel noticed was that it now had a big wall around it. The wall would keep out dangerous sea creatures such as sharks, but it also had a gate so that Ariel's friends could enter the lagoon. In fact, Flounder, Scuttle, and Sebastian were there to greet her.

"Isn't this a great idea?" Scuttle asked. "I helped, you know."

Ariel was thrilled. "Oh, Eric! I love it!"

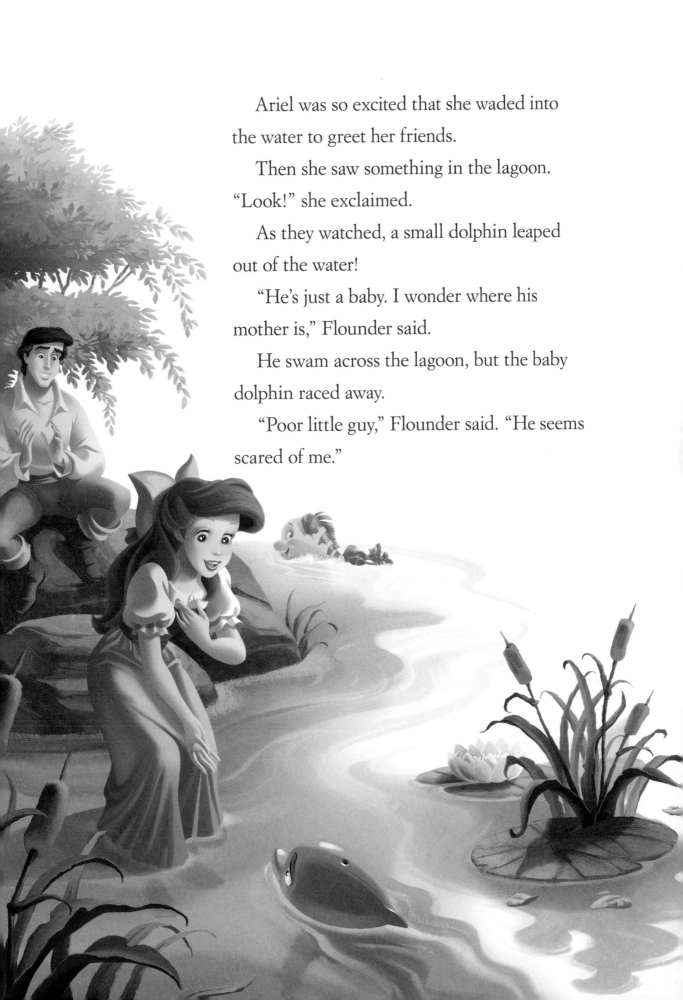

Ariel was so excited that she waded into the water to greet her friends.

Then she saw something in the lagoon. "Look!" she exclaimed.

As they watched, a small dolphin leaped out of the water!

"He's just a baby. I wonder where his mother is," Flounder said.

He swam across the lagoon, but the baby dolphin raced away.

"Poor little guy," Flounder said. "He seems scared of me."

But the princess wouldn't give up. Soon she had coaxed the baby to swim over to her.

"I wish there was something more we could do," Ariel said.

"I bet his mother is on the other side of that wall. Don't worry," Flounder said. "We'll find her!"

But a few days later, Sebastian and Flounder still hadn't found her.

"This is terrible," Sebastian said. "We have looked everywhere under the sea, but cannot find the baby's mother. What should we do?"

Ariel looked at the little dolphin. Tomorrow she would ask more of her friends from under the sea to help search.

Later that night, Ariel awoke to the sound of thunder. From the palace, she saw big waves crashing on the shore.

Eric joined her. "Are you worried about that baby dolphin?" he asked.

"He must be terrified," Ariel replied. "We need to go to him."

Eric followed Ariel into the stormy night. When they arrived at the lagoon, Flounder was trying to calm the frightened baby dolphin.

Ariel climbed onto the lagoon wall and called to the sea creatures. "Help me, please! I am Ariel, princess of the seas. I need my father, King Triton."

A whale was the first to respond. Then a school of fish flashed their fins.

"Thank you!" the princess shouted.

Below the surface, sea creatures raced to find King Triton.

Ariel returned to Eric. "I know my father will be able to help," she told him.

While they waited, Eric jumped into the sea and led the dolphin to calmer waters.

Suddenly there was a flash of light! King Triton had arrived.

The storm quieted down. The baby dolphin's mother was at the lagoon gate, frantically trying to get in.

"Oh, dear!" Ariel exclaimed. "The gate won't open! She can't get in!"

Eric looked at King Triton. "Do you mind?"

"Not at all," he replied. "Swim back, everyone!" He raised his trident and blasted down the wall.

The dolphins swam to each other, then the baby went to Triton to thank him.

That night, the moon rose. But there was no royal ball at the palace. Instead, Eric and Ariel returned to the lagoon.

The baby dolphin and his mother swam up and playfully splashed the prince and princess.

"I think that means we are forgiven!" Ariel said with a laugh.

She was glad that all of her friends were gathered together for a quiet evening—including her new dolphin pals.